Zoë
and the
Fairy Medicine

For Emily

First published in Great Britain in 2005
by Piccadilly Press Ltd,
5 Castle Road, London NW1 8PR
www.piccadillypress.co.uk

Text designed by Louise Millar
Colour Reproduction by Dot Gradations Ltd UK
Printed and bound in China by WKT

ISBN: 978 1 85340 811 3 (hardback)
978 1 85340 816 8 (paperback)

3 5 7 9 10 8 6 4 2

A catalogue record of this book is available from the British Library

Jane Andrews has two sons and lives in High Wycombe in Buckinghamshire.
Piccadilly Press also publish the other books in this series:

Zoë and the Tooth Fairy
Zoë and the Fairy Crown
Zoë and the Witches' Spell
Zoë and the Dragon
Zoë and the Magic Harp
Zoë and the Mermaids
Zoë and the Unicorn
Zoë and the Wishing Star

Zoë
and the
Fairy Medicine

Jane Andrews

Piccadilly Press • London

"I'll be away for a few days at the annual fairy convention," announced the Fairy Queen one morning. "There must be no trouble here at Fairy School."
The fairies assured her that they would be on their best behaviour, and watched as she flew off, clutching a very full suitcase.

A few days later Zoë and Pip were playing with their friend
Marcy in the woods. They were jumping from one toadstool
to the other. It was great fun!

Suddenly, Marcy jumped too high, and bumped her head on an overhanging branch.

Splat! She fell to the ground.

"Oh, poor Marcy!" said Pip.
"We must take her to see the fairy nurse immediately,"
said Zoë.

At the castle sick room, Marcy was put to bed with a bandage
on her head. The fairy nurse gave her some medicine to make
her feel better – but just as she was about to put the medicine
back she noticed something on the bottle.
"Oh, no! I've given her the growing medicine!" she cried.

Just then, Marcy's legs and arms started getting longer . . .

"Help," whispered Marcy.

"Oh dear . . ." said the fairy nurse, looking in the cabinet, "I'm afraid that we have run out of shrinking medicine, and only the Fairy Queen knows how to make it."

Zoë and Pip knew that in the library there was a book of potions and medicines and their ingredients, so they rushed there immediately. They had to stop Marcy from growing!

After searching all day, they found a recipe for Shrinking Potion. "*Eureka!*" cried Zoë. "But we will have to fly to the top of Fairy Mountain for some of these ingredients, and the mountain is guarded by a scary troll!"

They went back to say goodbye to Marcy, who had grown a
lot more during the day.
"Don't worry, Marcy, we'll shrink you again. We will be
off to get the ingredients first thing tomorrow," said Zoë.

Early the next morning, armed with Sleeping Dust to protect themselves against the scary troll, Zoë and Pip set off. They flew higher and higher into the mountains, up through the clouds and over the craggy rocks. They were very frightened and worried and tired, but they knew they had to keep going.

When at last they reached the top, they paused to catch their breath.

Thud! Thud! Thud!

As they were resting, they heard a sound like thunder.
"We must stay calm," said Pip. But the noise kept getting
closer and louder.

"*Thud! Thud! Thud!*"

"It isn't thunder at all," whispered Zoë as she and Pip clung to
each other, "it's . . ."

". . . the Troll!"

And just as the fairies were about to throw the Sleeping Dust
at him, the troll gave them a big, friendly smile.
"Can I help you, fairies?" he asked, most politely.
Zoë and Pip were speechless. The troll didn't seem scary at all!
"Have you had a long flight?" he asked. "Why have you come?"

Zoë was the first to find her voice. "Please, Mr Troll, our friend Marcy keeps growing and we need to make some Shrinking Potion, because the fairy nurse got mixed up and gave her a growing potion, and soon she'll be too big for the castle . . ." As Zoë continued to tell the story, Pip handed the list to the troll.

"Don't worry," the troll said gently. "I can help, but I'll need your assistance in getting all the ingredients."

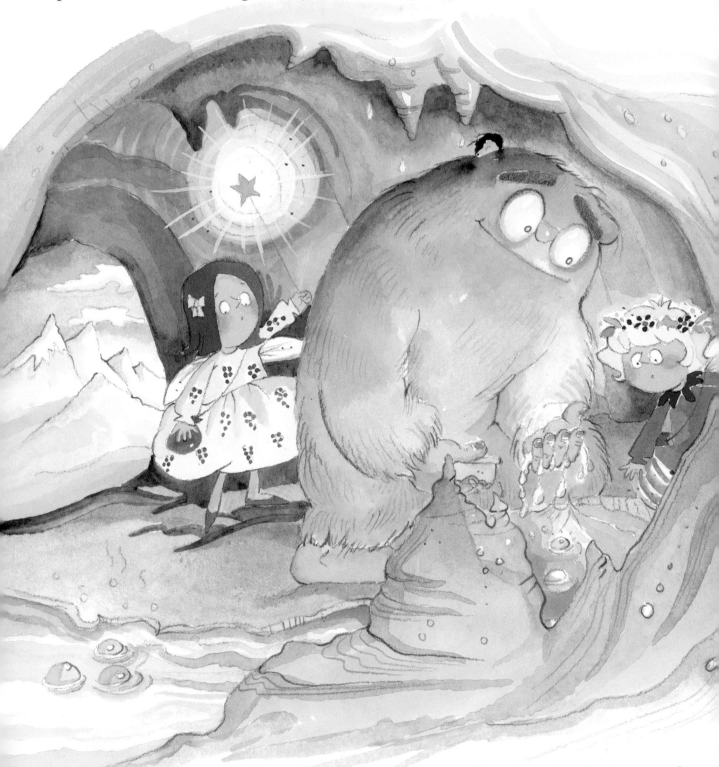

With that, the fairies were off with the troll to begin their search. First, they collected gooey slime from the troll's cave . . .

then they plucked a feather
from a sleeping vulture . . .

picked the deepest purple
forest violets . . .

and took some sticky
soft web from an
angry spider.

Back in his cave, the troll added
spices and seasonings . . . and at
last, he pronounced it ready.

It had been a long day, and Zoë and Pip were exhausted, so the troll kindly carried them down the mountainside.

The fairies at the Fairy Castle were so frightened when they saw the troll that they barred the windows and doors.

"Don't worry," Zoë and Pip called to them from the ground.
"We have the shrinking medicine – and the troll helped us!"

When Zoë and Pip were let in to the castle, they took the
potion straight to the sick room.
"Here – take this potion quickly," said the fairy nurse to Marcy.
"The Fairy Queen is coming back tomorrow morning!"
Zoë, Pip and the fairy nurse nervously watched and waited.
Then suddenly . . .

When the Fairy Queen returned,
she looked around carefully.
"Is everything in order?" she asked.
Everyone nodded yes.

"Isn't Marcy just a bit taller than usual?" asked the Fairy Queen.
"Er . . . She must have had a growing spurt while you were away," said Zoë.

"Hmmm . . . " said the Fairy Queen.
And when no one was looking she gave the troll a wink.